P9-AGA-714

Welcome Home, Mouse

Elisa Kleven

TRICYCLE PRESS
Berkeley

www.randomhouse.com/kids

Library of Congress Cataloging-in-Publication Data

Kleven, Elisa.
Welcome home, Mouse / Elisa Kleven.
p. cm.
Summary: Stanley, who is very clumsy, accidentally smashes Mouse's house, then promises to try to make a new one.
[1. Dwellings—Design and construction—Fiction. 2. Clumsiness—Fiction. 3. Mice—Fiction.] I. Title.

PZ7.K6783875Wel 2010
[E]—dc22
2009032302

ISBN 978-1-58246-277-6 (hardcover)
ISBN 978-1-58246-364-3 (Gibraltar lib. bdg.)

Printed in China

Interior design by Tasha Hall
Cover design by Toni Tajima
Typeset in Duality and Bembo Schoolbook
The illustrations in this book were created in mixed media collage with watercolors, ink, pastels, and colored pencils.

1 2 3 4 5 6 – 15 14 13 12 11 10

First Edition

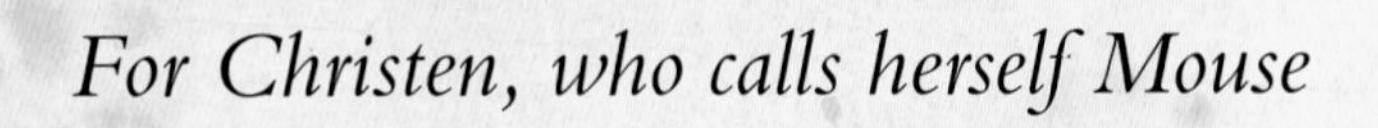

For Christen, who calls herself Mouse

Stanley was trying to help Mom make pizza, but SLOSH he spilled the oil, SPLOOF he sprayed the flour, SPLAT he tipped over the bowl of tomato sauce.

"Stanley," said Mom, "why don't you go out and play with your ball?"

"But I want to help," Stanley said.

“Okay, then,” said Mom. “Run to the grocery store for more tomatoes.” She handed Stanley her shopping bag, some silver coins tucked safely in the pocket. “Buy yourself a treat at the bakery with the change.”

Stanley bounded off, tossing
his ball. Up it soared . . .

down it crashed.

"My house!" cried a mouse. "My cozy house. Smashed to bits and pieces."

"Oh, Mouse!" said Stanley. "I'm sorry!"

"Where will I eat my meals?" asked Mouse. "Where will I sleep tonight?"

"I could make you a new house," offered Stanley. Mouse frowned. "I don't think so," she said.

"I could try," Stanley said.

"What kind of house could you make?" asked Mouse.

Stanley thought about that. "A surprise house?"

"Could you try to make it now?" asked Mouse.

"First I have to buy some tomatoes," said Stanley. "Why don't you come along?"

Stanley held out Mom's shopping bag, and Mouse crept into the pocket.

“Hi, Stanley,” said the grocer, whisking a crate of eggs out of the way. “What can I get you today?”

“Some tomatoes, please,” said Stanley.

“I’ll put them in a box this time,” the grocer said, “so they won’t get crushed on the way home.”

“A box—thanks!” said Stanley.

"This box gives me an idea," Stanley told Mouse.

"What's your idea?" asked Mouse.

"You'll see," said Stanley. "I hope it will work. But first let's get a treat."

"Hi, Stanley," said the baker. "Why don't you wait outside while I get your snack? Remember last time, when you toppled that wedding cake?"

Stanley blushed. "I'll have a blueberry muffin," he said, "and a bottle of apple juice, please."

Stanley broke the muffin in half so he and Mouse could share.

"Delicious!" said Mouse, dusting crumbs from her fur. "I only wish I had my little plate to eat it on."

"Me too," said Stanley sadly.

"You didn't mean to break it," said Mouse, offering Stanley the doily from their muffin like a handkerchief. But instead of drying his eyes with it, Stanley popped it into Mom's bag,

along with his bottle cap and paper napkin.

"Another idea?" asked Mouse. Stanley smiled. "Lots!"

As Stanley skipped home, new ideas fluttered and swirled through his head, bright as leaves.

"More surprises for Mouse!" he thought, adding flowers, twigs, and lacy moss, acorn caps and walnut shells, and one smooth, speckled stone to his collection.

“And here are more surprises!” thought Stanley, sifting through the recycle bin on his front porch. Into the bag went a small cardboard box, some stamped envelopes, and the lid of a jelly jar.

Mom came to the door. “You’re back! Here, let’s have those tomatoes.” She reached into the lumpy, bumpy, bulging bag. “What’s all this?” she asked.

“Careful, Mom,” said Stanley, “there’s someone inside.”

“Yikes!” Mom cried. “Who are you?”

“This is Mouse,” said Stanley. “My ball accidentally wrecked her house.”

"Where will you live?" Mom asked.

"Stanley has an idea," said Mouse.

"And it's a surprise," Stanley said, "so don't peek."

Stanley emptied the shopping bag. Then carefully, very carefully, he did some snipping,

and gluing,

and arranging,

and filled the tomato box.

Fresh Homegrown
Tomatoes
17
DANMARK
6
National Parks Centennia

"Here you are, Mouse," said Stanley.

"What a house!" cried Mouse. "What a lovely surprise of a house. All this time I thought you were—"

15
30
2ND
17
DANMARK

"Clumsy, I know," said Stanley.

"Clever," said Mouse.

"Kind," added Mom. "Now who wants pizza?"

Stanley served Mouse a piece, bubbly and warm, on her sturdy new plate.

"Welcome home, Mouse."